Bedtime!

Christine Anderson

Illustrated by
Steven Salerno

Philomel Books • New York

PHILOMEL BOOKS

A division of Penguin Young Readers Group. Published by The Penguin Group.
Penguin Group (USA) Inc., 375 Hudson Street, New York, NY 10014, U.S.A.
Penguin Group (Canada), 10 Alcorn Avenue, Toronto, Ontario, Canada M4V 3B2
(a division of Pearson Penguin Canada Inc.)
Penguin Books Ltd, 80 Strand, London WC2R 0RL, England.
Penguin Ireland, 25 St. Stephen's Green, Dublin 2, Ireland (a division of Penguin Books Ltd.)
Penguin Books India Pvt Ltd, 11 Community Centre, Panchsheel Park, New Delhi - 110 017, India.
Penguin Group (NZ), Cnr Airborne and Rosedale Roads, Albany, Auckland, New Zealand
(a division of Pearson New Zealand Ltd).
Penguin Books (South Africa) (Pty) Ltd, 24 Sturdee Avenue, Rosebank, Johannesburg 2196, South Africa.
Penguin Books Ltd, Registered Offices: 80 Strand, London WC2R 0RL, England.

Published simultaneously in Canada. Manufactured in China by South China Printing Co. Ltd.
Design by Cecilia Yung and Katrina Damkoehler. Text set in 18-point Lucida Casual.
The art was done in watercolor, gouache, and ink.
Library of Congress Cataloging-in-Publication Data
Anderson, Christine, 1961-
Bedtime! / Christine Anderson ; illustrated by Steven Salerno.   p. cm.
Summary: When Melanie is too busy playing to get ready for bed,
her mother gives the special bedtime treatment to the dog,
and Melanie misses some of the best parts of the routine.
[1. Bedtime—Fiction.] I. Salerno, Steven, ill. II. Title.
PZ7.A5235Be 2005   [E]—dc22   2004009460
ISBN 0-399-24004-7
1 2 3 4 5 6 7 8 9 10
First Impression

For our Melanie—C.A.

For James R. and Karen M.—S.S.

Melanie, it's time for bed."

"In a minute, Mom. . . .
I'm busy!" Melanie answered.

Mom poked her head in the room.
"Melanie, it's time for bed, now," she said.

"Just one more minute, Mom.
I'm very, very busy."

Melanie was building a tower
for animals to live in.

One minute passed.
Then another.
Then another.

"Well," sighed Melanie's mother, "*someone* has to get ready for bed. How about you, Bart?"

Melanie didn't notice them leave.
Her tower still needed more blocks.

Melanie stepped back and admired
her tower. Hmm, she thought, it still
needs something else . . .

"I see you want to play!" said Mom.

"Okay, just this once, though."

"Aha!" said Melanie.
"An elephant house!
In case elephants come over
to play. I must make it BIGGER!"

"All dry!"

said Mom.

Melanie looked at her tower. It was
spectacular! She even had a name for it:
The Very Spectacular Melanie Tower.
She made a sign that read ELEPHANTS WELCOME.

"Now, let's brush your teeth."

Melanie tilted her ear
toward the bathroom.
Was that her mother talking?
Who was she talking to?

"Such *lovely* hair," Mom said
as she brushed out the tangles
and tied a pretty ribbon.

Melanie peeked into the bathroom.
"Hey!" she said. "That's MY ribbon."

Mom seemed not to have heard Melanie.
"Here are your favorite pajamas,"
Mom said to Bart.
"You look just like
a princess!"

"Those are MY pajamas," Melanie grumbled. "*I* look like a princess in them."

"Now here's Daddy to give you a BIG good-night kiss."

Melanie always loved Daddy's
big good-night kisses.

"Time for a bedtime story.
Let's read your favorite!"
said Mom.

Bart jumped up onto Melanie's bed.
Melanie ran to the bathroom and
quickly brushed her teeth.

Now pajamas! She had already
missed having her hair brushed,
missed getting her pretty ribbon,
and *missed* Daddy's
big good-night kiss.

She didn't want to miss her
favorite part of the bedtime story, too!

Mom finished reading the story.
The room was quiet.

"Did you enjoy it, Bart?" she whispered.
But when Mom looked down, Bart was already
fast asleep.

And, curled up beside him,
so was Melanie.

It had been a busy, busy day.